KT-469-201

This book belongs to

Louise Large♡

The Story of the
DANCING FROG

Published in 2017 in Great Britain by
Barrington Stoke Ltd
18 Walker Street, Edinburgh, EH3 7LP

www.barringtonstoke.co.uk

Text & Illustrations © 1984 Quentin Blake

The moral right of Quentin Blake to be identified as the
author and illustrator of this work has been asserted in
accordance with the Copyright, Designs and Patents Act, 1988

All rights reserved. No part of this publication may be
reproduced in whole or in any part in any form without the
written permission of the publisher

A CIP catalogue record for this book is available
from the British Library upon request

ISBN: 978-1-78112-591-5

Printed in China by Leo

This book is in a super readable format for young readers
beginning their independent reading journey.

Quentin Blake

The Story of the
DANCING
FROG

Barrington Stoke

"Tell me another story about our family," said Jo.

"I'm really too tired, lovey."

"If I make the cocoa and the sandwiches."

"Well – all right then. What have I told you? Uncle Geoffrey and the Iceberg. And Sarah and her Lions. Do you know about Great Aunt Gertrude Godkin and the Dancing Frog?"

"No. Can I have that, please?"

"You get the cocoa and I'll see how much I can remember.

"When Gertrude was a young woman she married an officer in the navy. He was very handsome, with a black beard and a smart uniform.

"The trouble with being married to a sailor is that he has to go with his ship, so that a lot of the time you can't be with the person you most want to be with. Anyway, they were happy when they were together, and they had a house by the sea and Gertrude would watch for his ship returning, and when he came home he brought her presents from abroad."

"What sort of presents?"

"Little brass tables with folding legs, wooden camels, ornamental daggers.

"One day the ship didn't come back.

Gertrude waited and waited. Then there

was a letter from the navy to say that
the ship had sunk and Gertrude's sailor
was drowned. You can imagine how
awful it must have been to get a letter
like that."

"Yes."

"She went out of the house and started walking along by the river. There can't have seemed anything in life worth living for, and she was on the point of throwing herself in, so that she could be drowned too, like her husband, and finished.

"But she noticed something which stopped her. On one of the lily-pads in the river was a frog. It was dancing.

"Gertrude stood and watched it as it danced and then – I don't think she quite knew why – she walked into the water and picked up the frog and carried it home.

"That night Gertrude kept the frog in a bucket in the kitchen, and the next day she dug a pond for it in the garden. For the rest of the day Gertrude stayed by the pond, watching the frog swim about. From time to time it would do a little dance on the grass.

"That evening, after she had had something to eat, Gertrude put a record on the wind-up gramophone she had been given as a wedding present. Then she went out into the garden and picked up the frog in her hands and brought him in and put him on the kitchen table. And the frog slowly started to do a new kind of dance – a dance to the music.

"And then we don't know quite how it happened – but the frog went on the stage. Perhaps Gertrude knew someone at the local theatre – and a dancing frog is a rather unusual thing. And no doubt

Gertrude didn't have much money after her husband disappeared and was glad of anything they could earn. Anyway, for the first time the frog's name appeared on a theatre poster. Right at the bottom – GEORGE, THE DANCING FROG."

"Was that his name then?"

"I don't know. Maybe it was just his stage name. After that they travelled about the country, wherever they could get work. It must have been a hard life for Gertrude – carrying the luggage, staying in cheap lodgings, arguing with landladies who didn't want a frog in their rooms.

"But they made lots of friends. At one theatre George took part in the conjuror's act. He dived through a hoop and then the conjuror made him disappear.

"At another theatre he jumped out of a hat when the comedian pretended to be drunk."

"What Daddy used to call squiffy."

"Yes, that's right, lovey. George learned lots of new dances – the Lancers, the Gay Gordons, the Polka.

"And then one day Gertrude was told something that changed their lives – there was a job at a big theatre in the city. A talking dog had been taken

ill with a sore throat and they were
desperate for a replacement. George
got the job. He did all his dances and
suddenly everybody wanted to see him.

"It was a different life. People sent flowers to George's dressing room, and waited to see him at the stage door. Newspaper reporters interviewed Gertrude about him. Society hostesses wanted him at their parties.

"George was taken to expensive restaurants. A famous chef even invented a dish specially for him, of worms in butter sauce."

"Ugh. Fancy cooking worms."

"They weren't cooked. Frogs won't eat anything that's dead. They were alive.

"At least they weren't poor any longer – but there was even more work for Gertrude. Arranging about the money they were to be paid – arranging about trains, arranging about luggage. But it must have been exciting,

travelling around the world ... strange
cities, warm nights under starry skies.

"In Paris George danced with a girl dressed in feathers, and the audience went wild with excitement.

"He also did a wonderful dance with another girl who waved shawls.

"He danced with Spanish dancers and you could hear his croaking above the sound of the castanets.

"In Russia he danced in a special version of 'Swan Lake'. He jumped higher than any of the ballet dancers.

"It was in Monte Carlo that Gertrude had her offer. An English lord asked her to marry him.

"'This is no life for a woman,' he said. 'I have a house in the country and another in London, and everything shall be provided for you. Leave all this and live with me as Lady Belvedere.' It must have been a great temptation.

"Who was to know how long George

would go on being successful? But they

were just getting ready for their tour
of the U.S.A., and somehow she knew
she couldn't really give up. So Lord
Belvedere had to be content with No for
an answer.

"The dreadful business of the fire happened in New York. George was rehearsing a new musical. The night before the show opened the hotel where they were staying caught fire.

"Gertrude was out in the street buying the evening papers. She saw smoke bursting out of the hotel doors and windows. How could she possibly get back to George, who was in their room on the thirteenth floor? Then suddenly she saw him on the window ledge by the open window.

"By then the fire-engines had arrived. Gertrude snatched a bucket of water from a fireman and called out at the top of her voice.

"It must have been the most extraordinary thing he ever did, on the stage or off it. A 120-foot jump into a bucket of water with perfect precision.

"George went on that night and was more brilliant than ever. At the end of the show the audience stood and applauded for twenty minutes.

"And it went on like that. Nobody much remembers them nowadays but they really were a great success."

"Was Gertrude ever sorry that she didn't marry Lord Belvedere?"

"I don't think she ever told anybody she was."

"She preferred the frog."

"Well, I suppose you could say they looked after each other over the years."

"And what happened to them in the end?"

"The last time anybody in the family saw them was before the war. They had a little house in the South of France, with a water-tank for George.

"Gertrude used to grow hollyhocks and sort out their newspaper cuttings. In the warm weather she would give George a shower with the watering-can."

"And are they dead now, then?"

"Well, that was a long time ago, so I suppose they must be."

Jo collected up the cocoa mugs and the plates.

"Was that a true story?"

"More or less."

"But frogs don't really dance, do they?"

"Not normally, no."

"And no one could really catch a frog and put it on the stage."

"You can do all kinds of things if you need to enough."

"Yes, I suppose so."

Draw like Quentin

Quentin Blake's pictures look sketchy and quick, full of energy and movement. But did you know that Quentin draws a very careful rough version of each picture, and then uses a light box to draw it again for a special sketchy feel?

The watercolour paper

The rough

Light box

pens & ink

Illustration from *Words and Pictures* (Tate Publishing, 2013) © Quentin Blake, 2000

Our books are tested
for children and young people by
children and young people.

Thanks to everyone who consulted on
a manuscript for their time and effort in
helping us to make our books better
for our readers.